Music Player
Storybook®
written by Wendy A. Wax

Contents

Reader's Digest
Children's Books®

Pleasantville, New York • Montréal, Québec • Bath, United Kingdom

Play Song 1

Beauty AND THE BEAST

Belle in: A Love Uncovered

Play Song 2

Belle was spending a cozy afternoon reading by the fire. She had to admit that the Beast kept some interesting books around. Across the room, the Beast was feeling sorry for himself. "I was a fool to think a girl as beautiful as Belle might fall in love with me," he muttered.

"Cheer up," said Mrs. Potts, the teapot. "Give it time."

Just then, Belle burst out laughing. The Beast thought he had never heard such a lovely laugh. He turned to see what she was reading.

"That's my favorite book!" His eyes lit up. "Can you believe the evil dragon decides to go to school to become a princess?"

Belle laughed in agreement. "My father would love this. I miss reading to him in the evenings. Would you mind if I read to you?"

"I...I'd love that," said the Beast, and Belle began to read.

Play Song 3 The next afternoon, the Beast asked Belle to go for a walk with him. She remembered the nice time they'd had together the day before. "Of course," she said. "It'll be good to get some fresh air."

"Have fun!" called Lumiere and Cogsworth.

Belle hadn't been outside the castle much since she'd arrived. The Beast took her arm.

"I can manage by myself," Belle said confidently.

Embarrassed, the Beast pulled his arm away. Suddenly he felt shy and awkward.

The Beast walked ahead of Belle, not noticing how she had to struggle to keep up with him. Then it started to snow. "You must be cold," he said. "Shall we head back?"

"I'm fine," said Belle, snuggling deeper into her warm cloak. "I love walking in all kinds of weather."

"You do?" asked the Beast, surprised at how alike they were. He slowed down so they could walk side by side. Belle put her hand in his. Before he could doubt himself, the Beast asked Belle to dine with him.

"I'd love to," said Belle.

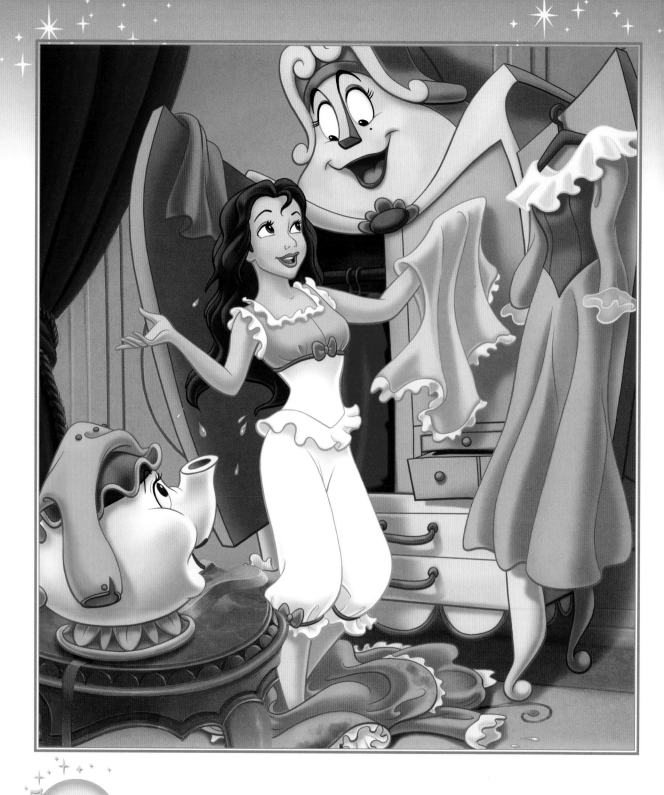

🎵 **Play Song 4** Belle couldn't decide what to wear to dinner. She didn't want to look too fancy. She just wanted to be comfortable. And Belle herself was beginning to feel more comfortable with the Beast....

"I like the orange gown," said Mrs. Potts.

"Me, too," said Wardrobe. "It brings out your dark hair and eyes, my dear."

"Then the orange gown it is!" said Belle, and she put it on.

Meanwhile, Lumiere and Cogsworth were in the Beast's chambers, helping him prepare for dinner. The Beast also wanted to look his best. Lumiere washed his fur, and Cogsworth trimmed it. The Beast began to hum his favorite waltz.

"I've never heard you hum before!" said Lumiere.

"A special song for a special girl, sir?" asked Cogsworth.

They hummed along with him as he dressed in the most splendid clothing he owned. Something special was in the air!

Play Song 5

At last, Belle came down to dinner. She was so beautiful, the Beast could only stare.

"Am I missing an earring?" Belle asked, reaching for her ear.

"Uh...no," said the Beast. "Would you...uh...like a buttered coal? I mean...."

"...a roll!" Belle said, giggling, "I'd love one."

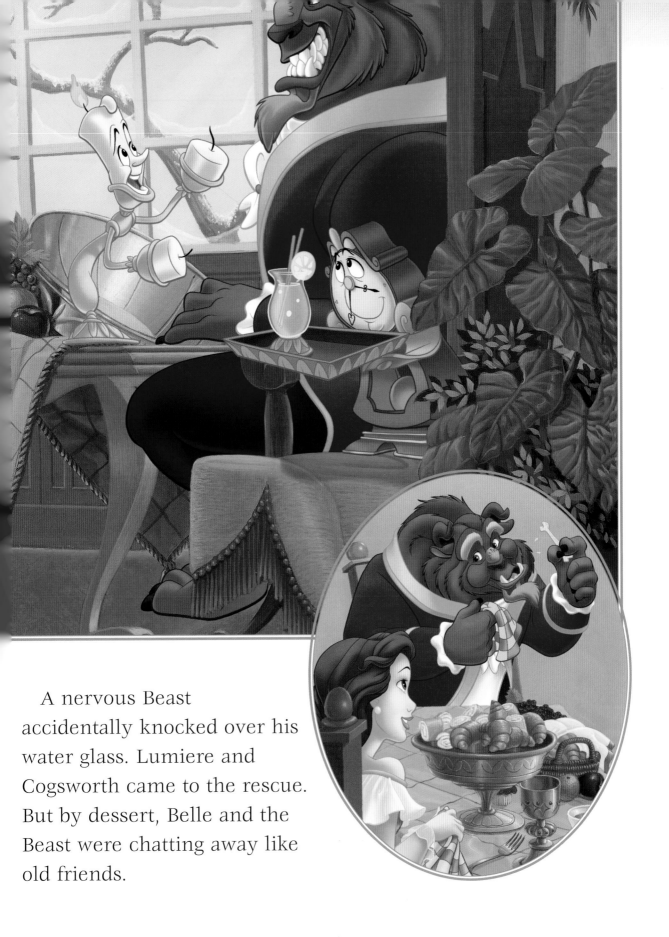

A nervous Beast
accidentally knocked over his
water glass. Lumiere and
Cogsworth came to the rescue.
But by dessert, Belle and the
Beast were chatting away like
old friends.

She couldn't stop thinking about the Beast. He didn't act like a beast at all! He was so kind and gentle. And they could talk about everything for hours and hours without ever getting bored.

At that moment, Belle realized that she truly cared for the Beast. Might he, too, have special feelings for her?

The next day, Belle couldn't find the Beast anywhere. She wondered if she'd been wrong to think he might have special feelings for her. Finally, she asked Mrs. Potts where he was.

"He's busy preparing for tonight," said Mrs. Potts.

"Tonight?" asked Belle.

"The Master has a special evening planned," said Mrs. Potts. "Just the two of you."

Belle's heart fluttered. She envisioned herself descending the staircase in a lovely gown of...not that it mattered. She knew that it was what's inside that counts.

Play Song 7 That evening, after a romantic, candlelit dinner, the Beast led Belle to the dance floor. The Beast felt confident and comfortable as he led Belle around the room, staring into her eyes. Belle stared back, feeling happy and secure in the strong arms of the Beast.

THE LITTLE MERMAID

Ariel in: The Music of Love

"I have a surprise for you!" Flounder said to his best friend, Princess Ariel. He grabbed her hands and started to swim in circles.

"I love surprises! What is it? Give me a hint, Flounder," said Ariel.

"You won't believe it. It's so amazing, I need a band of buglers just to announce it! Follow me."

But Sebastian objected. After all, they were in the middle of a rehearsal for his latest musical extravaganza, and Ariel was the lead singer. "Where are you going?" he called after them.

"It's just a five-minute break," reasoned Ariel. "Flounder has something he needs to show me." She flashed him a smile.

"Unbelievable!" muttered Sebastian. "Young people these days don't know about work...."

Play Song 3

Flounder led Ariel over to a statue of a handsome human he had found on a shipwreck. "Ta da!" he said.

"Prince Eric!" Ariel exclaimed. "I love it!"

"You mean you love *him*," said Flounder.

"Shhh," said Ariel. "You're the only one who knows. If my father finds out, he'll be furious."

She swam around the statue, taking in every detail. She imagined gazing into the dreamy eyes of Prince Eric. She had only seen him once on a sinking ship. He probably had no idea that she had been the one to save him from drowning.

"Ariel, shouldn't you be getting back to rehearsal?" Flounder asked. But Ariel's mind was elsewhere. She imagined marrying Prince Eric. In order to walk down the aisle, she'd have to get herself a pair of legs and feet. They'd have a romantic wedding at the water's edge so her family could be there to watch. Her father, King Triton, would be there, smiling proudly—after all, this was only a daydream. Her older sisters would be there, too. She wondered how the prince's family would feel about having merfolk as relatives. Some humans, she'd been told, didn't believe they existed. But if Prince Eric loved her, so would his family.

"Ariel!" Sebastian called from several feet away. "Come back!"

🎵 Play
Song
4 But Ariel was planning the menu and didn't hear anyone else. First, they would serve trays of whipped seaweed on crackers and blue sea-grass wraps. She hurried through the soups, salads, and main courses, so she could get to the best part—the wedding cake. It would be huge and pretty, with tiny statues of herself and Prince Eric.

"Yoo hoo! Ari-ellll!" called Sebastian. "We must rehearse!"

♫ **Play Song 5** He didn't get an answer because Ariel was busy deciding what to wear to her wedding. After much thought, she decided on a shimmering veil, a tiara, and yellow sea stars in her hair. She imagined Flounder bringing her strands of pearls that he borrowed from the most distinguished family of oysters.

"There you are!" Sebastian said, swimming toward Ariel. "I'm not going to let you get away this time."

"Sebastian!" Ariel said, finally hearing him. "If we don't swim fast, we're going to be late for my wedding."

"Huh?" said Sebastian, feeling very confused. "Wedding?"

🎵 **Play Song 6** "What's going on?" asked an orchestra member.

"Ariel thinks she's having some sort of wedding," grumbled Sebastian. "I guess we could hold the rehearsal here." But before he could give them the signal, Ariel cleared her throat. She had an announcement to make.

"I, Ariel, take Prince Eric to be my lawful, wedded husband," she said happily. "I love him with all my heart."

Flounder couldn't help gazing at Ariel with admiration.

♫ **Play Song 7** "You make a beautiful bride," he said. "Prince Eric is the luckiest human in the world."

Even Sebastian felt teary-eyed as he led the orchestra in a fantasy-wedding musical number.

"Now will you sing, Ariel?" an exhausted Sebastian pleaded with her. "Please?!"

"I have one last thing to do," said Ariel. With that, she flung a bouquet of seaweed. Flounder swam to catch it.

Sleeping Beauty

Aurora in: A Dream Come True

Princess Aurora had never been so happy in her life. She was about to marry Prince Phillip, the dearest, most handsome man she had ever met, and the man who had been promised to her since the day she was born. Prince Phillip also happened to be the man of her dreams—really! She remembered the day in the forest when they first met....

Aurora had been singing to her animal friends about her dream of falling in love with a handsome stranger. Prince Phillip, who happened to be nearby, was enchanted by her angelic voice and set off to find her. As soon as Aurora and Phillip looked into each other's eyes, they felt as if they'd known each other forever. It was true love.

Play Song 3

"Princess Aurora!" said the courtier, calling her back to the present. "I'm afraid I need you to go over the list for your engagement party."

"Oh!" Aurora said, feeling a bit embarrassed as the prince and the courtier hovered nearby. "Oh, dear!" she said, going down the list. "There's so much to do! My dress is ready for a fitting. The flowers need arranging. And the cake—what shall we do about the cake?" There was no time for daydreams any longer. It was time to get down to business.

Play Song 4

Aurora wanted so much to bring her special touch to all the arrangements, but she'd need just a little help. It wasn't long before the good fairies—Flora, Fauna, and Merryweather—were on the job. With their magic, they seemed to be everywhere at once!

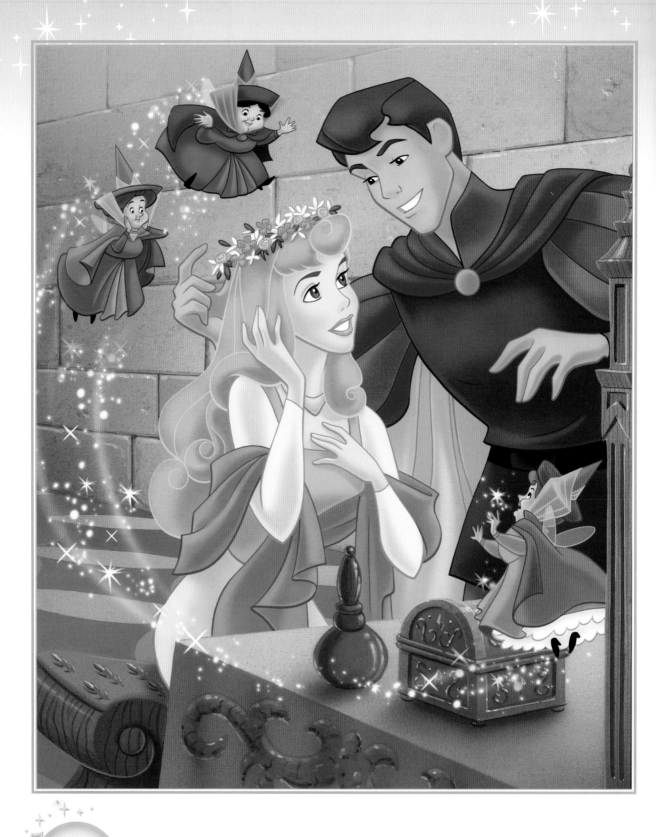

♫ **Play Song 5** At last, the day of the party arrived. Prince Phillip surprised Aurora in her dressing room.

"You brought me a garland of flowers from the woods!" exclaimed Aurora. "How perfect!"

"They're to remind you of the time we first met." Prince Phillip smiled as the good fairies made their final adjustments and arranged the garland to their liking.

Just before the party, Princess Aurora stole the prince away for a few minutes. "I have something for you," she said, leading him to the wing of the castle they'd be living in after their wedding.

As they went inside, Prince Phillip looked around happily. "Whoever decorated this has exquisite taste," said the Prince. "It's very similar to my own."

"I decorated it, silly," said Princess Aurora, delighted at the Prince's reaction. "This is my wedding gift to you."

"You know me so well," said the Prince, falling even more in love with Aurora. "We're going to have a happy life here."

"I couldn't agree more," said Aurora.

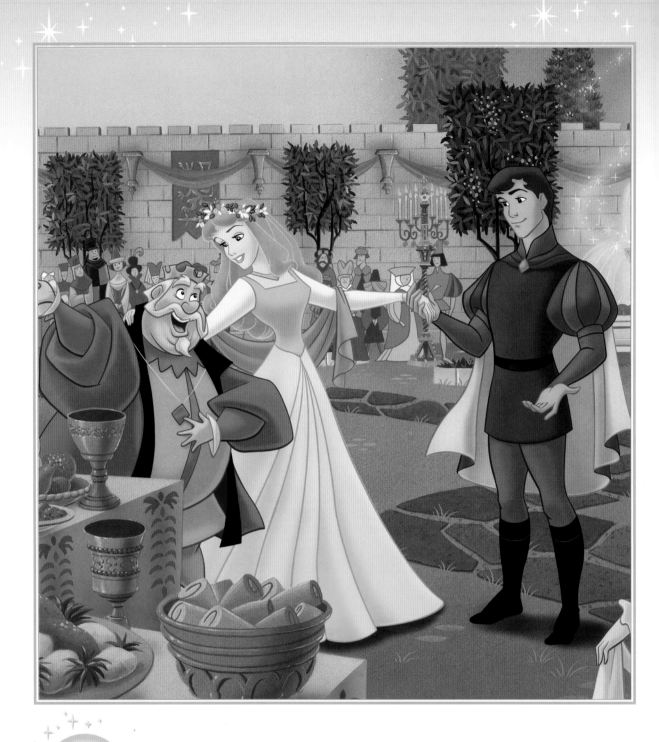

Play Song 6

At last, they headed off to the party. Aurora and Phillip were delighted to greet so many guests. And everyone agreed that the engagement party was the best they had ever been to. It was everything it should be—classic and elegant, festive and fun.

"May I have this dance?" Prince Phillip and his father, King Hubert, asked Aurora at the exact same time. Princess Aurora's face shone with happiness.

"Go ahead," said King Hubert. "Watching the two of you together makes me happy."

Play Song 7

Princess Aurora and Prince Phillip danced till all the guests went home. Only the forest animals remained, for they knew that a promise made long ago had been fulfilled in the loveliest way. There was definitely magic in the air!

Cinderella

Cinderella in: The Best Intentions

This guest list does seem to go on forever." Cinderella gave a sigh to her friends the mice. Though she loved the Prince with all her heart, she did not love preparing for her royal wedding.

"Gus—Gus help Cinderelly?" asked Gus.

"Just don't let all this royalty change me into someone I'm not," Cinderella told him.

Cinderella's lady-in-waiting, Prudence, helped choose a gown, but Cinderella was horrified by her taste. "I look silly in frills...." But Prudence was too busy to listen.

Play Song 3

Meanwhile, Jaq and Gus went to find some help—Cinderella's Fairy Godmother.

"We worried about Cinderelly," Jaq told her.

"She not looking forward to her wedding," said Gus.

"I thought she loved the Prince," said the Fairy Godmother.

"Thassaright!" said Jaq. "But too many royal rules to follow!"

Play
Song
4
The Fairy Godmother agreed to help. "That gown
does make you look rather like a wedding cake. Would
you like me to whip up a simple, elegant dress for you,
just like I did for the ball?"

"Oh, yes!" exclaimed Cinderella.

♪ **Play Song 5**

"Anything else?" she asked.

"I'm responsible for the invitations," said Cinderella. "But I can't do it alone, and I can't count on help from my family."

"*We're* your family, dear," came the reply. *Poof!* The guest list was transformed into a thousand invitations, which were sent out immediately.

34

"Oh, no! The wedding cake!" Cinderella gasped. "I should have ordered it yesterday!"

"How about today?" asked her Godmother. Then—*poof!* There was a wedding cake. *Poof* again! Cinderella was wearing a lovely, elegant gown, just like her Fairy Godmother had promised.

Play Song 6

On her wedding day, Cinderella felt happy and relaxed—thanks to her Fairy Godmother and friends. They waited with her as she prepared to walk down the aisle. At last it was time to go.

"Remember to smile!" came Prudence's whispered reminder from behind the scenes—not that Cinderella needed to be reminded. She had plenty to smile about now.

As she walked down the aisle, in glass slippers adorned with hearts, the crowd gazed at her with admiration and awe. They had never seen such a beautiful bride. "I must admit her gown is prettier than the one I chose for her," Prudence said to herself.

Cinderella didn't notice anything around her. All she saw was the handsome Prince she was going to share her life with.

🎵 **Play Song 7** "How does it feel to be a princess?" the Prince murmured in Cinderella's ear later that evening.

"Amazing," Cinderella murmured back. "But that's because you're my Prince." She winked at her Fairy Godmother and waved to the mice as she whirled past them on the dance floor.